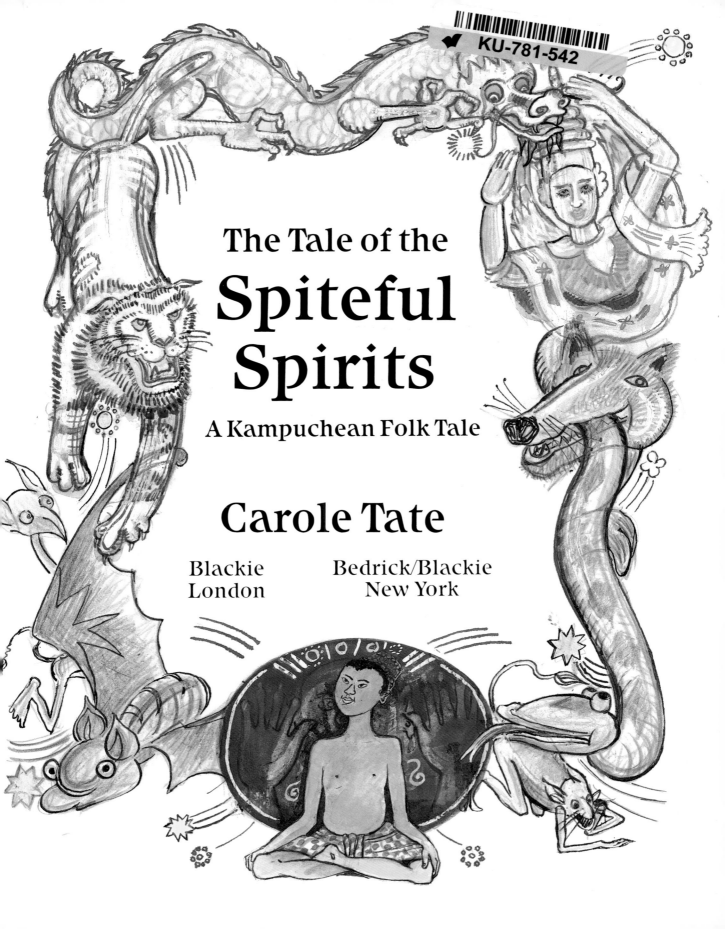

The Tale of the
Spiteful
Spirits

A Kampuchean Folk Tale

Carole Tate

Blackie
London

Bedrick/Blackie
New York

Many years ago, in a far Eastern country
called Kampuchea, there was a young boy
who lived with his rich uncle. Every night the boy
looked forward to the old family servant re-telling
ancient tales of tigers and foxes, dwarves and dragons,
which had been passed on by word of mouth for many
years. The boy's friends begged him to repeat
the stories, but selfishly he never would.

Thanks to Anne for her help with the story

Copyright © 1991 Carole Tate
First published 1991 by Blackie and Son Ltd

A CIP catalogue record for this book is available
from the British Library.

ISBN 0-216-93066-9

Blackie and Son Ltd
7 Leicester Place
London WC2H 7BP

First American edition published in 1991 by
Peter Bedrick Books
2112 Broadway
New York, NY 10023

Library of Congress Cataloging-in-Publication Data
Tate, Carole
Tale of the spiteful spirit/Carole Tate. — 1st
American ed.
Summary: Because a young man will not pass on the
stories he is told by an old servant,, the spirits of the
stories, having nowhere to go, live in a cramped
leather bag, where they plan a spiteful revenge for
the young man on his wedding day.
ISBN 0-87226-445-9
[1. Folklore—Cambodia.]   I. Title
PZ8.1.T1617Ta] 1991
398.21'09596—dc20
[E]   90-41949
                                                CIP
                                                AC

10 9 8 7 6 5 4 3 2 1

Printed in Hong Kong

Because the boy refused to pass on the tales to others the forlorn spirits of the stories were left with nowhere to go. They ended up forced to live in an old forgotten leather bag, and once inside they could not get out. Every night a new spirit was imprisoned, and soon the bag became overcrowded and uncomfortable. The spirits grew angrier and angrier.

As the years passed, the old servant continued to tell his stories every night. The boy grew into a young man and the time came for him to marry. His uncle arranged a fine match for him with a pretty daughter of a rich family from the next village.

The day before the wedding the old servant was tending the stove when he heard strange whisperings coming from the young man's bedroom.

'So he's getting married now is he,' muttered one.

'He's going to be so happy,' complained another.

'And we've been ss-shut in here s-ssso long,' hissed a third.

'We must plot our revenge,' they all shrieked.

Astounded, the old man rushed outside.

He crept as quietly as he could round the side of the house and peered through a window into the young man's bedroom. It was difficult to see but he could just make out the old leather bag twisting and turning upon its nail and he could hear the voices coming from within it.

'I have a plan,' said a husky voice from inside the bag. 'I shall disguise myself as a deep well. He will want to quench his thirst during the wedding procession and I shall poison the water.'

'If that fails,' said a syrupy voice, 'I will be a field of strawberries at the roadside—he need eat only one strawberry and he will have terrible stomach-ache.'

Then a harsh voice added, 'I will become a red-hot poker and hide myself in the bag of rice husks they use for dismounting. What a nasty shock he'll get!'

'And just in case that fails, I will be a snake and creep under the bride's mat to bite him,' hissed the last and most venomous voice.

The old man was horrified. He knew he would have to act alone to thwart the story spirits' revenge, for he was sure no one would heed an old man's warning.

At dawn the next day the wedding procession made ready.
Everyone was wearing their best clothes. The old man
begged to be allowed to lead the bridegroom's horse.
The uncle reluctantly agreed. And so they set off,
the bridegroom leading, followed by the villagers
carrying a scarlet palanquin ready for the bride.

Everyone was amazed at how fast the old man led the bridegroom's horse and before long they were all feeling hot and thirsty. When they came upon a clear well with a drinking gourd attached to it, the bridegroom asked the old man to stop so he could have a cool, refreshing drink. But the old man ignored him and marched even faster, straight past the well.

Next, a tempting field of strawberries came in sight.

'Please stop,' gasped the bridegroom. 'I would love one of those red strawberries.'

But the old man took no notice and kept on going quickly down the road. The attendants and the uncle were all very angry and the uncle made up his mind to scold the old man when they arrived at the wedding.

At last the wedding party reached the bride's house.
Everyone was tired and thirsty. A servant came forward
with a sack of rice husks for the bridegroom to dismount
upon. To everyone's surprise the old man rushed up and
kicked the sack away, so that the bridegroom stumbled
and fell. The uncle, now beside himself with rage, decided
the old man should be punished.

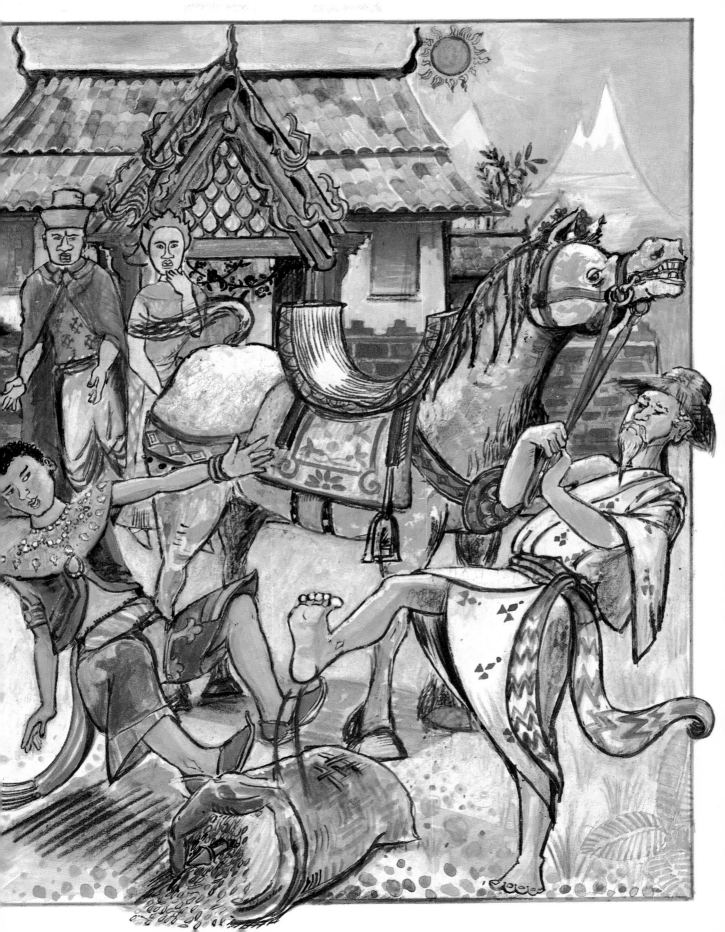

As he entered the house with
the bride's father, the bridegroom
saw that a splendid banquet had
been prepared. Exotic meats and
fruits lay on gleaming dishes.

The bridegroom stood at the
table and waited until his bride
and her attendants appeared
from behind a dragon screen.

The bride took her place beside her future husband and the wedding began. The couple took a sip from the wedding cup and everybody cheered. Now the feasting could begin and the tumblers, clowns and dancers could start to perform. Everybody was enjoying themselves except the old man. Only he knew that there was still one more danger to come.

After much feasting and celebrating, the last guests finally departed and the house fell silent. The young couple were alone in their room talking quietly of their future when there was a violent banging on the door. In rushed the old man waving a sword. He whipped back the carpet. Coiled menacingly underneath was a large snake. Without hesitation the old man struck it again and again until it lay dead.

Now at last the old man was able to explain the revenge of the story spirits. When everybody saw the scorched rice husks with the poker in the middle, and the body of the dead snake, they were all convinced of the truth of his story. The old man was rewarded handsomely by the bridegroom's uncle.

The bridegroom was sorry for his selfishness. He promised to release the imprisoned spirits by telling the stories to his bride and later to his children.

And so, the stories were once more passed on from father to son, from mother to daughter, brother to sister. The spirits were never to be imprisoned again.